KU-714-694

Bite and mackay

Go to Sea!

Cathel Hutchison

Illustrations by Ingebjorg Smith

Published by Really Wild Press

ISBN 978-0-9955444-1-3

Meiklejohn's Croft

Lamington

Invergordon

Ross-shire

IV18 OPE

Scotland

Copyright © Really Wild Press 2017

All rights reserved. This book or any portion thereof may not be reproduced or used in any manner whatsoever without the express written permission of the publisher except for the use of brief quotations in a book review or promotion material.

This book is dedicated to
my father and to my grandfather

'Wake up whitey Bite!
Out of bed woolly Mackay!'
said Isabel Macnamara.

'Stretch your legs and clean out your ears.

Today we're off to sea!'

'Och, what are we off to see?'
grumpy-growled Mackay. 'I've got howling
practice today with the Portkelpie Dog Choir.'

'I can't go to sea and leave my toys at home!'
yip-yawned Bite.

'**Avast ye landlubbers!**' laughed Isabel.

'Don't you know that the sea is full of fat-bellied trout? Eat one and your belly will be full for a week!'

'**Fat-bellied trout?**' Mackay licked his lips. 'Three of those will make a good snack!' And he jumped from the couch down **to the floor.**

Bite was already at the door.

Isabel and her husband Ian led the boys outside, and then put on their leads.

'Let me off!' yelped Bite tugging on his lead.

Mackay rolled and kicked.

'Wheesht boys!' shushed Ian.
'It is only a five minute walk to the harbour.'

Fifteen minutes later, Isabel stopped the crew at the harbour, beside their fine old wooden sailing boat, Muc Mhara.

Then Isabel put on her Captain's cap and she became Captain Macnamara.

'All aboard Muc Mhara!'

'Lifejackets on,' said Ian, holding a dog-sized lifejacket in each hand. 'One for Mackay,' who squeezed in and didn't even squirm.

'One for Bite,'

who twisted and turned like a wriggling **worm.**

Put-put-put-put!

Captain Macnamara started the engine.
'Untie the ropes and prepare to leave port!'

Ian jumped to obey.

'We're rrrr-off!'

howled Bite and Mackay
with a growly hooray.

MUC MHARA

'The wind is with us,'
said Captain Macnamara.

'Hoist the sail!'

'Aye-aye Captain!'
saluted Ian.

'I'll help!' yipped Bite.

'The sail is caught!' complained Ian.
He gave it a big **heave**.

Up **whooshed** the sail and Bite as well.

'Oh Bite!' tutted Ian.

'I know you want to help, but today please watch
and learn. One day you might become the
skipper, but not if you tear my sail!'

Bite yipped and leaped down,
landing on cushiony Mackay.

'Get off me!' Mackay's grumpy-growl turned into a hippo-wide yawn. 'Oh-wow! I am going to sleep until lunch.'

'Well, I am going to hunt for fat-bellied trout!' yipped Bite.

'Save three for me...' snored Mackay.

Bite stared out to sea and spotted his
own wavy reflection.

'It looks like me, but swims in the sea,' he thought.

'It must be a fat-bellied trout!'

Whoosh!

A blast of wind
filled the sail, heeling
Muc Mhara over on
her side. Curious Bite
lost his seat and
plopped overboard.

Mackay was having a scary dream. In it he was being chased by fat-bellied trout.

A loud **splash** woke him up from his troubled sleep.

'Save me from the fat-bellied trout!'

he whimpered and leaped from the deck into the sea.

'Dogs overboard!' yelled Ian.

'Calm down dear!' said Captain Macnamara. 'I will turn Muc Mhara about. You fetch a long rope and a big, juicy bone.'

Splish-splosh!

Bite and Mackay were lost overboard.

'**Yowwww!**' gurgled Bite. '**Let go of my tail!**'

'I can't swim!' glugged Mackay.

Just then, the boys heard a cry of 'Bone!' followed by a splash.

'Is that a bone?' yipped Bite.

'**No!**' grumpy-growled Mackay. '**That's a bone-fish!**' and he dived on it in a black woolly flash.

High above, a scheming skua watched the boys
with their prize.

Shrieking he swooped down to snatch it for himself.

Bite spotted the dive-bomber first.

'I'll hold the bone-fish, you defend me!'
he yipped, grabbing onto one half of the bone.

'No! I'll hold the bone-fish!' grumpy-grumped
Mackay, grabbing onto the other half.

Just as the boys were arguing, the bone jerked in their grasp and was h a u l e d away through the waves.

Whoosh!

Scheming skua missed them by a feather and instead swallowed a beak-full of salty seawater.

Back on Muc Mhara, Ian pulled on the emergency bone-on-a-rope, and landed Bite and Mackay on deck like two hairy mackerel.

'What brave sea-dogs!'

said Captain Macnamara when the boys were wrapped up, warm and cosy.

Mackay gave a growl and Bite chased his tail. The boys liked praise, but preferred a slice of ham.

That evening,
back in Portkelpie,
Mackay sat outside
the Macnamara's
cottage.

'Arooooo!'

he howled at the
glimmering moon.

'Arooooo!'
the Portkelpie Dog
Choir joined in too.

Inside, Bite curled up on his favourite seat, beside his mountain of toys.

The boys had had a long and eventful day. They had set sail out to sea and lived to tell the tale. Maybe on their next adventure they would spot a fat-bellied trout, and definitely help to sail!

Cathel Hutchison

Ingebjorg Smith

Cathel Hutchison is an
editor and ecologist based in the
Highlands. This story was
inspired by the real-life
adventures of mischevious
hounds, Whyte and Mackay.

Ingebjorg Smith is a fine artist
and illustrator. She began
her career illustrating for
the Dòtaman series on CBBC.

Also available in Gaelic as *Fire agus Faire a' dol gu muir* at

www.biteandmackay.co.uk

978-0-9955444-0-6